THE DELUXE NOVELIZATION

randomhousekids.com

ISBN 978-0-7364-3440-9

Printed in the United States of America

10 9 8 7 6 5 4 3 2 1

THE DELUXE NOVELIZATION

Adapted by Victoria Saxon

Random House 🏠 New York

1

Queen Elsa was working quietly at her desk when the bells in Arendelle's clock tower began to chime. It was noon.

Elsa put down her pen and went to the window.

Her little sister's birthday was just weeks away, at summer solstice, and Elsa wanted to plan something wonderful, something perfect, to make up for all the years Anna never had a real celebration. But what?

Throughout their childhood, Anna

had never really had a birthday party. Elsa remembered that her little sister had once stood on the other side of Elsa's bedroom door and begged Elsa to come out for a small birthday dinner. But back then, Elsa had been hiding her magical icy powers. She had accidentally hurt Anna with them once and, worried that might happen again, had cut herself off from her sister and the rest of the kingdom until a year ago.

That was when Elsa's icy powers had been revealed—and Anna had helped Elsa gain control of them.

Now the sisters were happy, and there were no more secrets. The castle and the entire kingdom of Arendelle was a much happier place, and she and Anna were learning so much about each other. Every day with Anna held new surprises.

Suddenly, Elsa had an idea.

"That's it!" she said to herself. "We'll give Anna her first surprise birthday party ever!"

Elsa began the preparations right away. There would be gifts, guests, and a cake. For the gifts, she could get Anna a new dress and new shoes. She could get her a new pillowcase, and—

Shoes? Pillowcase? Elsa put down her pen. There had to be something more, something Anna would love, something special.

Elsa decided to ask Gerda and Kai for ideas. The two faithful servants had been with the royal family for years and knew both girls well.

"How about a family portrait?" Gerda suggested. "It could be commissioned especially for Anna's birthday."

Elsa clapped her hands happily. It was a great idea . . . until she realized that their family was only the two of them.

But the idea was still good. Elsa wondered if she could find an old family portrait in the castle attic. Perhaps she could have it cleaned and dusted and touched up by the royal portrait artist.

As Elsa started up the stairs, Anna peeked into the hallway.

"What are you doing? Do you want some help?" Anna asked. It seemed as though Anna had popped up out of nowhere.

"Um, no thanks!" Elsa replied.

But Anna kept insisting.

"I don't need help," Elsa said. She just needed time to search the attic—without Anna.

"Okay!" Anna still didn't leave.

"Tell you what," Elsa said, "why don't you go into the attic for me? And I'll go . . . finish my royal duties."

"Okay!" Anna said. "Oh, what am I looking for?"

Elsa paused, trying to think up some reason she might be looking through the attic. "String!" she said finally. "I was hoping to find a ball of string."

Anna went up to the attic. It was filled with antiques, old trunks, and lots of dust and spiderwebs. But where was a ball of string?

Meanwhile, Elsa headed downstairs. She felt guilty for fibbing to Anna, but maybe it wasn't really a fib. She probably did need string. For something.

Elsa quickly left the castle and headed into the village. At least she knew what to do about the cake.

At the town bakery, Elsa asked the baker to keep her special order a secret. "It's for Anna's surprise birthday in a few days," she explained. "I want her to have the best birthday cake ever, and I've heard your ice cream cake is the best in Arendelle."

The baker nodded. He was a slight man with a sprout of black hair at the top of his otherwise bald head.

"What flavor do you want?" he asked.

"Chocolate," Elsa said firmly. She knew for a fact that Anna loved chocolate.

"Ah, a chocolate cake for Princess Anna!" the baker exclaimed. "Would you like dark chocolate, milk chocolate, or white chocolate? We could do a chocolate fudge sauce or a chocolate mocha icing or perhaps a chocolate cream topping with chocolate sprinkles?"

Elsa paused. She had thought chocolate was chocolate! She had no idea which kind Anna loved best.

Just then, the bell on the baker's door jangled, and in walked Anna. She was covered in dust and carrying a huge ball of string. She had followed Elsa.

"Elsa? Look what I found! I mean, this is a lot of string," Anna said. She looked around the shop. "What are you doing here?"

"Um, I was . . ." Elsa saw a box of cupcakes. "I was tasting a cupcake."

"What a great idea!" Anna said. "Why didn't you bring me along?"

"Please, won't you have a cupcake, too, Princess Anna?" the baker asked. "I know you love chocolate, but *which* kind of chocolate do you like best?"

The baker looked at Elsa. He was trying

to find out Anna's favorite chocolate. Elsa smiled in gratitude.

Then Anna winked at Elsa.

"We'll try one of each, and please mix up the icing, too," Anna said. She wanted Elsa to try everything.

The two sisters laughed as they walked home together. There would be lots of cupcakes at the castle that night, but Elsa still didn't know which kind of chocolate to choose for Anna's birthday cake.

Elsa continued working on Anna's surprise party, but it was hard to keep such a big secret from her little sister. Anna turned up everywhere she went.

One morning, Elsa sneaked out of the castle before Anna awoke. She wore a cloak with a big hood as a disguise, in case Anna went searching for her later. She was hoping to find just a few more birthday gifts for her sister.

But in every shop, Elsa kept finding gifts that seemed good for Anna—she wanted to share them all! She visited a jeweler, a livery stable, and a tailor. She watched a glassblower work, saw a craftsman twist strands of silver jewelry together, and stood by as a weaver's loom clacked. She even trekked up to Wandering Oaken's Trading Post & Sauna to see what items Oaken might have for a princess.

By the time she returned to the market, Elsa had to sit down.

"Elsa?" Kristoff said. He had spotted Elsa on a bench, bundled up in her cloak. "Are you okay?" Kristoff had become a

good friend to Anna and Elsa, along with Sven the reindeer and Olaf, a happy-go-lucky snowman who loved warm hugs. The group had shared some big adventures over the past year, and they enjoyed spending time together.

"Just tired, that's all," Elsa replied. "Finding birthday gifts for Anna is fun, but it takes a while."

Kristoff nodded, and so did Sven, standing behind him. "I know you want to show Anna how much you care about her," Kristoff said. "But you don't have to do it by yourself. Let me and Sven help!"

Elsa smiled. It was really nice to have friends. She handed Kristoff a list and then watched as he and Sven headed to the shops in the marketplace.

As Elsa sat there feeling grateful for her

friends' help, she heard a rich, sweet sound coming from a nearby school: children singing. The harmonies were some of the loveliest Elsa had ever heard.

The queen walked to the front gate of the school and peered inside to see where the choir was rehearsing. She felt a tug on her sleeve. A little girl was standing next to her, with her mother close behind.

"Say 'excuse me,' dear," the mother prompted.

"Excuse me," the girl said. "I'm late for choir practice. Are you going inside, too?"

"No, not today," Elsa replied.

"My name's Kirsten," the little girl said. "We're practicing to sing for Queen Elsa and Princess Anna someday. At least, we hope to. I want to sing for the queen, but I also want to sing for Anna. Do you like Elsa or Anna

better?" She waited patiently for a response.

Elsa smothered a smile. Apparently her cloak and hood were a very good disguise! "I like Anna," she said.

"Okay," Kirsten said, and she skipped through the gate.

Laughing to herself, Elsa watched the little girl disappear inside.

As her birthday approached, Anna began to feel a little lonely. Elsa was almost always in her office, working. Kristoff was busy, too. Anna had barely seen either of them for at least a week.

On the evening before her birthday, Anna found herself pacing in the throne room and explaining the situation to Olaf.

"I love thrones," Olaf said. "Do you think I can sit on it?"

"Go ahead," Anna said. She helped the

little snowman up into the seat. Then she continued her story. "I just hope I see my friends tomorrow. I'd hate for the day to go by without my best friends."

"What's tomorrow?" Olaf asked innocently. "Is something special going on?"

Anna had to smile. "Well, it's my . . . It's the summer solstice. It's the longest day of the year."

"That *is* special!" Olaf agreed. "What do you do on the summer solstice?"

"Good question," Anna said. "I guess we could do summer solstice things."

"And what are summer solstice things?"

Anna thought for a moment. "I think we should do something nice for our friends. To celebrate."

"Can we start tonight?" asked Olaf.

"That's a great idea," Anna said. "You

know how Kristoff likes to keep his sled polished and clean?"

"Yeah!" Olaf shouted. "But what does that have to do with us?"

"Well," Anna said, smiling, "maybe we could *wash* his sled. It's been in storage for a while, and it's probably dusty."

As Anna and Olaf made their way to the kitchen, the castle seemed remarkably quiet. Anna found a big bucket by the sink and started filling it with water.

Suddenly, Gerda and Kai walked through the kitchen doors carrying several, large, full trays over their heads. But the moment they saw Anna, they began to back out.

"Oh!" Gerda said.

"Hi!" Anna said. "Can you help me—"

"Terribly sorry," Kai said quickly. "We just, uh—we turned into the wrong room."

He stammered, trying to sound natural. The trays held an assortment of fancy eclairs for Anna's birthday, and he didn't want the princess to see. "We just have to . . . turn around now. Bye!"

Gerda and Kai disappeared down the hallway, their trays still held very high.

"That was odd," Anna said, watching them leave. She turned back to her bucket and added soap.

"Mmmm," Olaf said. "That water looks perfect for a warm bath. I've always wanted to try a bath."

"Sorry, Olaf, not this time," Anna said with a smile. "Now let's go!" She lugged the big bucket of warm soapy water out the door at the back of the kitchen. Olaf followed happily.

Making their way around the side of the

castle, they entered the stable. They found Kristoff's sled in one of the stalls. It was covered with a big blanket.

Anna grabbed a corner of the blanket and was about to yank it off when she heard a grunt. Then a snort. She pulled back the blanket and saw Kristoff sleeping on the sled's front bench. Sven was draped over the back. The two had been working so hard on Anna's birthday preparations that they had fallen asleep right there.

"Whoa!" Anna exclaimed.

"Huh?" Kristoff startled awake. "Who's there?"

Anna took a step back.

Olaf answered happily, "Me, Olaf! And Anna!"

"Oh, wow! Hey!" Kristoff said. "What are you doing here?"

Anna tried to explain. "Well, I was going to—um, well, I was going to wash your sled. As a surprise, for the summer solstice—"

"Summer solstice?" Kristoff stepped down from the wagon seat. "That's a very important day." He put the bucket of sudsy water to one side, then took Anna by the arm. "Come on. Let's go outside."

They walked out into the dark and sat on the side of a wall. Olaf followed, also looking up into the night sky. It was beautiful and full of stars.

Kristoff looked at Anna. "I know it's the summer solstice tomorrow, and it's a very important day. Because it's your birthday."

"Anna's birthday?" Olaf cried. "That's so exciting!"

"Well," Anna said, "it's not that big a deal. Just another year, right? I mean, it was a big year, but still." Anna smiled and shrugged.

"On your birthday," Kristoff said, "you're supposed to do something special."

"Exactly," Anna said. "That's why I was trying to wash your sled."

"No," Kristoff replied. "You're supposed to do something special for *you*."

"But I don't need to do anything special," Anna said.

Kristoff shook his head. "Just because you've never had a real birthday—"

"Yes, I have! I've had lots of birthdays," Anna interrupted. "I always eat in the formal dining room, and—well, that's it."

"Do you even know what a real birthday is?" Kristoff said.

"Ooh! Ooh! I know!" Olaf said. He raised his little twig arm in excitement. "Real birthdays are so much fun—at least, that's

what the little trolls told me. Family and friends get together, and there are candles and everyone sings and there are presents, and—"

"Yes, presents are good," Kristoff said. "I remember one year, Bulda gave me a stalagmite."

"I may have had that kind of birthday once, a long time ago," said Anna. "I don't really remember."

Sven snorted and nudged Kristoff.

"Point is," Kristoff said, "songs and presents are nice, but they're not what make a real birthday." He cleared his throat. "A birthday is—"

"What?" Anna asked.

"Well, a birthday is a day when everyone gets to say that they really, really—uh—love—uh. Oh, boy. They get to say how much they—" Kristoff was blushing.

"—love cake?" Anna finished. "That really *is* a great day!"

"Yeah," Kristoff said, relieved. "You're right."

From her window in the castle, Elsa looked down and saw Kristoff talking with Anna.

"Thank you, Kristoff," she whispered. He was keeping Anna busy.

Elsa turned to her dresser and pulled out the ball of string Anna had retrieved from the attic. It was significantly smaller now, but there was still quite a bit of string left. Elsa picked it up and got back to work. There were only a few hours left till Anna's birthday, and for the first time in weeks, Elsa felt that she truly had everything in place.

It was very early and still dark when Elsa awoke the next morning. She shook off her tiredness and smiled when she realized this was *the* day: Anna's birthday!

She quickly dressed and hurried down to the castle's kitchen. A lot of preparation had already gone into making the day a spectacular surprise, and Elsa wanted to make sure everything was perfect. For the first time, her sister would get a wonderful birthday celebration. Elsa couldn't wait!

Olina, the chef, was awake and cooking breakfast for everyone in the castle. "Good morning, Your Majesty! Would you like something hot to drink?"

"Not for me, thank you," Elsa said, "but I bet Kristoff would like some breakfast. Have you seen him? He said he'd help set up in the courtyard."

"He stopped by just a few minutes ago. He wanted carrots for Sven."

"Excellent," Elsa said. Happy that Kristoff was already awake, she grabbed a big mug of tea and a bowl of oatmeal to take to him.

Outside, the stars were just starting to fade as Elsa headed toward the stables, where Kristoff usually fed Sven in the morning. The big reindeer seemed at home there. Elsa's feet crunched on the fresh hay, and the scent tickled her nose. When she got to

Sven's stable, she knocked on the door.

"Kristoff? I have breakfast. Are you there?"

She heard some rustling inside.

"Elsa? Hold on just a second!"

"Kristoff, is everything all right?"

Suddenly, the door swung open and Sven charged out, his eyes rolling wildly. He was dripping wet, with soap bubbles clinging to his fur. Then he shook himself.

"Sven, stop!" Kristoff cried. But it was too late. Water splattered everywhere. "So sorry," he told Elsa with a sigh.

Elsa looked at Kristoff. She couldn't believe her eyes. He was wearing a clean shirt and pants. His hair was slightly wet. Had he actually taken—

"Yup, I took a bath," he said. "And so did Sven. As you can see." Kristoff eyed her quizzically. "Why are you looking at me like that? We thought, you know, for Anna's birthday—"

"Shhh!" Elsa said, smiling. "Remember, it's a surprise! You do clean up really well, though."

Elsa headed outside. There wasn't much time left. She still had to make sure everything was ready for the surprise party.

Stepping into the large courtyard just outside the castle, Elsa was pleased to see that the preparations were moving along. She made a mental note to freeze the fountains as an extra decoration before she woke Anna. The courtyard looked very nice: colored balloons, tables with flowers, and streamers. Gerda and Kai were putting bright flowers into vases on every table. Everything was in place and looking festive.

Elsa glanced up at the sky. The sun was just peering over the rooftops and shining into the courtyard. Elsa wiped her brow. It did seem a little warm, but the icy fountains would help keep the courtyard feeling just right.

One thing was missing, though. Elsa glanced around in a momentary panic . . . until she saw the baker. Thank goodness! He had just delivered the birthday cake and was now assembling it and adding the final touches.

"I put chocolate ice cream into the mold first," he explained. "Then I added chocolate fudge sauce, and then the vanilla with the vanilla fudge sauce, and then the chocolate mousse, and then a layer of white chocolate with a hint of strawberry, and—"

"It's beautiful!" Elsa exclaimed. "I bet it's

tasty, too. Anna will adore this."

"Oh, yes!" the baker agreed. "We've got it covered, Your Majesty." Very carefully, he lifted the fourth and top layer onto the cake. Once the layers were in place, Elsa's powers would keep it cold until it was time to eat.

"Don't forget to come to the party later," Elsa called as he left. She gazed at the cake, taking it all in. The last part of the decoration was up to her.

"Okay, here we go," Elsa murmured. She waved her hand in the air, and as she did, icy magic swirled, encircling the top of the cake. A moment later, there was a little frozen statue of Anna at the very top!

It was beautiful, and it looked like Anna, but—

"So lonely," Elsa muttered. Again, she gave a flourish. The ice magic swirled, and

this time the cake topper became a little statue of Anna and Elsa standing together. But the sisters looked very formal.

"Stiff," Elsa said, frowning.

She started again, going for a likeness of the two sisters in an action pose. The magic glittered, and there it was, a little statue of Elsa hugging Anna, just as Anna was blocking a blow from—

With a gasp, Elsa realized she had just re-created the moment from a year ago, when Anna had let her body get frozen completely so she could save Elsa.

"No," Elsa said. "I can't do that!"

One more time, the queen changed the ice sculpture. Now the cake topper portrayed a scene of Anna and Elsa ice-skating happily. Nice, but was it appropriate for a birthday?

"Come on, Elsa!" she told herself. "It's for

Anna. You can do this." She raised her hand in the air again, ready to try something new.

"Relax," someone called out. Kristoff was perched on a ladder nearby. "It looks great." He and Sven were putting the finishing touches on a birthday banner. Sven was holding several buckets of paint on his antlers.

"I just want it to be perfect," Elsa said.

Elsa turned back to Anna's birthday cake and added some swirls to the sides, and icy flowers along the lower layers.

"Speaking of perfect, check this out!" Kristoff said.

He reached out to hang the last section of the HAPPY BIRTHDAY ANNA banner. The banner had multiple panels, and each one had a letter on it. The letters were strung together, and they hung sloppily on a straggly rope that

stretched across the entire courtyard.

Elsa gasped. There was paint splashed everywhere!

She quickly composed herself and walked over to Kristoff. After wiping paint off his face, she glanced at some paint dripping from the sign and onto the ground. There was a lot of cleanup to be done. "Kristoff, are you sure I can leave you in charge here?" she asked.

"Absolutely!" Kristoff replied. He glanced at his banner proudly.

"Because I don't want anything to happen in this courtyard," she added. She had worked so hard to prepare for the party. Everything needed to be perfect for Anna.

"What could happen?" Kristoff asked. "It's all set."

Just then, Elsa spotted Olaf standing next

to the birthday cake. He swiped his little twig fingers across the frosting.

"Olaf, what are you doing?" Elsa cried.

Olaf turned. "I'm not eating cake," he protested, though his cheeks were bulging.

Elsa frowned.

"But . . . but it's an ice cream cake," Olaf said, still looking hopeful.

"And it's for Anna," Elsa scolded. Olaf looked so sorry that it was hard to stay angry. Elsa sighed and walked away, freezing the fountains as she went.

Behind her, Olaf pulled the frosting out of his mouth and patted it back onto the cake.

4

Just then, the morning bells chimed. The sun was peeking over the high mountains that edged the fjord. It looked like the start of a beautiful day.

Elsa shivered, feeling excited. The big moment had finally arrived!

"Are you sure you've got this?" she asked Kristoff.

Kristoff nodded. "I'm sure."

"Don't let anyone in before we're ready!" Elsa called to Kristoff. She froze a gargoyle

on the side of the castle for good measure.

"I won't," Kristoff said. His hat and clothes felt itchy since his morning bath. He wanted to lean against a pillar and scratch—

"And don't touch anything!"

Kristoff blinked. "I'm just going to stand here," he reassured her.

"I'm probably going to walk around a little," Olaf announced. He loved seeing all the decorations, with all the frost and the icy things and the cake topper and the cake. . . .

"Keep an eye on that cake!" Elsa called back to Kristoff. Then she ducked inside the castle's main entrance.

Kristoff looked at Sven. He lowered his voice and pretended to speak as the reindeer: "She thinks you're an idiot."

"Well, clearly she's wrong," Kristoff said in his real voice. He turned back to work—

and slammed into the cake table. The cake teetered precariously.

"Ooh! Whoops!" he said, skipping back and forth with his arms outstretched, ready to catch the cake if it fell. Finally, the cake settled. "Everything's fine," he told himself in relief.

Nearby, Olaf was looking at Kristoff's handmade birthday banner. Each letter of HAPPY BIRTHDAY ANNA was flapping in the breeze. Olaf cocked his head as he studied the letters. He really wanted to read the banner, but it was hard. He squinted and tried to sound out each letter. Then he shook his head.

"I can't read . . . or spell," he concluded.

Kristoff relaxed a bit. He just needed to hold things together a little longer.

Elsa hurried along the castle hallway, finally reaching Anna's bedroom. Cracking open the door, she tiptoed over to her sister's bed. Anna was sprawled across her large mattress with her sheets tangled in a mess. Her mouth was wide open, and she was snoring loudly.

Elsa whispered, "*Psssst!* Anna."

Anna yawned and stretched her arms, but her eyes stayed closed.

"Yeah?" Anna mumbled, still half asleep.

"Happy birthday," Elsa said gently.

"*To you . . . ,*" Anna sang, automatically finishing the birthday song in her sleep.

Elsa smiled. "It's your birthday."

Anna opened her eyes groggily and sat up. "*To me . . . ,*" she sang again. Then she fell back onto her pillow. "It's my birthday."

"Come on," Elsa urged.

Suddenly, Anna's eyes flickered open. "It's

my birthday!" she exclaimed happily.

"Mmm-hmm. And it's going to be perfect." Elsa pulled her little sister out of bed.

Anna's eyes widened with happiness as Elsa led her to the closet. The first step was a brand-new dress. Elsa had worked with Arendelle's finest seamstress to create something extra special. She just hoped it would fit as perfectly as the seamstress had promised.

Anna gasped with delight when she saw her new dress. It was beautiful: a teal skirt decorated with bright yellow sunflowers, with a darker bodice featuring a flower design in the center. And on top of it all was a short jacket, covered with embroidered flowers.

"I love it!" Anna cried, twirling. "It's perfect for the summer solstice. Elsa, did you know that it's the summer solstice right now—

I mean, today?" She hugged the dress.

"*And* also your birthday!"

"I know, but this dress—it's perfect for both. I love the sunflowers!" Anna exclaimed.

"*Achoo!*" Elsa sneezed.

When she sneezed, two tiny snowmen popped into existence just behind her. Neither sister noticed as the two creatures spun in midair and tumbled to the ground. They scampered out the door.

"Bless you!" Anna said.

"Thank you," Elsa replied. Then, with a magical flourish, Elsa created a new dress for herself, too. It was a long, frosty, pale green gown.

"Whoa!" Anna said.

With a smile, Elsa waved her hand and added an icy glow to Anna's dress as well.

"Fancy!" Anna added.

This truly *was* her best birthday ever.

Then Elsa held up a piece of string that trailed onto the floor. She smiled and handed the end to Anna. "Just follow the string!"

"The string?" Anna stared. Then a happy grin grew across her face as she realized that it was part of her birthday fun.

She quickly followed the string out of her room and into the hallway. Elsa laughed, watching Anna crawl under a large chair and over a small table. The string kept going! Finally, Anna stopped at a suit of armor, where the string went right into the helmet.

Curious, Anna reached inside the helmet— and pulled out a beautiful sparkly bracelet.

"Woo! I didn't expect this!" Delighted, Anna placed the bracelet on her wrist. It fit her exactly. Of course it did. Elsa had planned everything.

Anna turned to hug her sister. This was turning out to be a wonderful birthday!

Elsa laughed. Then, with a mischievous smile, she pointed. And that was when Anna realized there was more string to follow! The birthday treasure hunt was not over yet.

Anna's heart raced. The string extended from the armor all the way down the hall. She ran to follow the string, slipping on the floor. She was having so much fun!

"Be careful!" Elsa laughed. "No need to rush." It was hard to tell who was more excited—Anna or Elsa.

Anna unraveled the string from a giant brass doorknob and followed it under a rug. She went into a hallway and saw that the string was wrapped around a small plant.

Anna followed the string into another room, where she found a huge armoire. It

had lots of drawers and knobs, and the string was wrapped around all of them. It was a trick to unravel everything, but the string finally led Anna to a small door at the top of the armoire. She opened it and peered into the dark space.

"Oh, look!" she cried. Inside was a little Olaf cuckoo clock! The clock began to chime as Anna pulled it out of the armoire. Suddenly, a tiny Olaf figure popped out of the clock. "Sum-mer!" it announced.

Anna giggled.

"Not finished yet!" Elsa said.

Anna picked up the clock and kept following the string. This time it led her out onto the balcony. There were sunflowers tied to the railing!

Elsa handed Anna a huge bouquet.

Anna was delighted. Then she saw

something. "Oops! Little bee," she warned Elsa.

Elsa turned. Her eyes went wide. A bee sting could ruin Anna's birthday. Elsa moved to shoo it away, and—

"Achoo!" she sneezed. *Well, that scared away the bee,* Elsa thought.

At the same time, several wriggling little snowmen appeared in the air and dropped off the balcony. Neither sister noticed.

5

Down in the courtyard, Kristoff was still working with Sven and Olaf.

Suddenly, Olaf gasped. A group of cute little snowmen was scurrying into the courtyard! Each one was made of a few small snowballs.

"Little brothers!" Olaf yelped happily. He reached out, scooped up a few of the little guys, and gave them a big welcoming hug. He didn't know where they had come from, but he loved them!

Kristoff eyed the snowmen doubtfully. "Olaf, I don't think they should be in here. We still have things to do for the party."

"But they're so little," Olaf replied, patting one of the snowmen on the head. "And I think they want to help!"

Kristoff didn't look convinced.

Inside, Anna and Elsa had already run all through the castle, following the string. Now they were outside, standing on a window washer's wooden platform.

The platform bumped against the side of the castle, very high up. The two girls held on to the ropes, grinning with excitement. Anna still had the string in her hand.

When she tugged on the string, a pulley brought up a picnic basket—with something yummy inside. Anna examined it more closely.

"Ooh, sandwiches!" Anna exclaimed, grabbing hold of the basket and pulling it onto the wobbly platform.

The wobbliness gave Anna an idea. She placed her foot on a pillar and pushed the platform away from the building. It was like a swing! "Woo-hoo!" she shouted.

"Whoa!" Elsa gasped. But then she kicked off, too. It was fun!

As the girls swung past a window, Anna glanced inside. "Look!" she cried. It was her room. "Gerda's tidying up my room! Oh, hi! Thank you!" She waved at Gerda and almost lost her balance. Luckily, Elsa steadied her.

Inside Anna's bedroom, Gerda thought she heard a voice calling from outside the window. She looked up and saw the tops of two heads—one with red hair and the other blond, swinging outside below the windowsill.

"Oh, my! KAI!" she hollered. She flung open the bedroom door and ran into the hallway. "I think I just saw Princess Anna and Queen Elsa outside the window!"

On the other side of the wall, the girls were laughing so hard, their stomachs hurt. They quickly worked the ropes and lowered the platform so they were out of sight.

"Hang on," Elsa said. She adjusted the pulley and lowered the platform all the way to the ground.

At the end, the rig slipped and the platform knocked into the ground with a *thump*.

Elsa's feet hit first, and the momentum sent her rolling onto the grass. Anna was right behind her, tumbling into a heap.

When they sat up, the window washer's rope dangled nearby, and the picnic basket was upside down on Anna's head.

They both giggled as Anna set the basket aside. "Hey, let's make snow angels in the grass!" Anna laughed. She spread out her arms, moving them over her head. When she stood up, there was an imprint in the grass.

"Hang on. I can help," Elsa said. She lifted her hands and created a little snow flurry over just the two of them. The sisters stretched out on their backs in the light, fluffy snow and made snow angels.

"This really is my best birthday ever." Anna reached into the picnic basket and pulled out her birthday sandwich. "Are you ready for lunch? I am." Anna took a bite. *"Befff!"*

"I know." Elsa reached for the other half. "Best sandwich ever! Right?"

"Umff," Anna said, her mouth still full.

6

$\mathcal{T}$he sisters sat side by side on the grassy slope, finishing Anna's birthday lunch. Then they lay on their backs again and looked up at the sky.

"Those clouds up there, see?" Anna said. They look like Olaf!"

"Oh! So do those ones!" Elsa pointed.

"Huh," Anna said. "They all kind of look like Olaf."

"Well, some of them look like Marshmallow," Elsa added, referring to the giant snowman she'd created to protect

47

her ice palace the previous year. Both girls laughed.

"We'd better get going," Elsa said, getting to her feet. She gave a little cough.

"Are you feeling all right?" Anna asked.

"I'm great!" Elsa replied. "Come on, let's go." She needed to keep Anna moving.

Anna's eyes grew wide with astonishment. "There's more?" she asked.

Elsa grinned. "Yup!"

Elsa held up the string again, and Anna laughed when she realized it was now leading them in a whole new direction.

After the picnic, Anna followed the string back into the castle, down a hallway, and, finally, to the royal portrait room. The birthday string went under the furniture and around and above each of the paintings.

"Wow! That's high. How did you get up there, Elsa?" Anna asked, climbing onto the back of a couch to reach a section of string.

"I have my ways," Elsa answered.

"Hmm." Anna teetered on her tiptoes, jumping a bit to pull the string down.

"I got it—whoa!" Anna fell, and so did a vase! But Elsa caught them both. "That was exciting," Anna said in relief. "Thanks." After she was back on her feet, she turned to Elsa. "Okay, really. How did you get the string so high?"

"If you must know," Elsa said in her most regal voice, "even a queen has to bounce."

"What?" Anna started laughing as she watched Elsa climb onto a long, cushioned settee. Then Elsa began jumping up and down! Anna quickly joined her. The two

bounced and laughed. As they bounced, Elsa pointed to one of the pictures.

"A family portrait!" Anna exclaimed, plucking the painting from high off the wall. Elsa had commissioned a new portrait of herself and Anna—plus Kristoff, Olaf, and Sven!

The sisters collapsed in the cushions, grinning at each other. "I love our family!" Anna said.

"Do you remember our last family portrait, with our parents?" Elsa asked.

That portrait was painted many years before. The royal artist had finished it just before the king and queen left on their final voyage. Back then, Elsa had been afraid that she might hurt someone and didn't want to leave her room. But their parents had insisted that she sit for the painting.

"Don't worry," the king had told Elsa. "Just wear your gloves." He and the queen sent the royal artist to Elsa's room. He painted her separately from the rest of the family.

"I remember when we sat for that portrait," Anna said. "Mama and Papa were so happy."

"I remember, too," Elsa said.

"I missed you."

"I missed you, too."

"Well, now our family has grown." Anna smiled. "And really, who else has a snowman and a reindeer in their family?"

"Nobody!" Elsa laughed, and it tickled her throat. *"Achoo!"* she sneezed. More little snowmen appeared and ran away.

"Elsa, I think you're getting sick," Anna said. "Maybe we should stop."

"I feel fine," Elsa replied. "Besides, you

still need to follow that string!"

So Anna picked up the portrait, along with the cuckoo clock, the bracelet, and the flowers. Her arms were full and she staggered a bit, but she followed the string.

The string led the girls around a corner to a bicycle.

"Ooh!" Anna cried in excitement. "Can we ride it? Indoors?"

"Why not?" Elsa climbed onto the bike. A moment later, a grinning Anna climbed on behind her, a little clumsily. It was hard to balance while carrying all her gifts.

Together, the sisters headed down the hallway, pedaling and laughing and trying not to tip over. The string was still leading them forward.

"Woo, this is fun! Where is the string going now?" called Anna.

The two sped right past her next gift: a colorful pair of silk stockings, hanging from the ceiling.

Elsa leaned on the handlebars and spun the bike around. She ducked under the stockings—and they flapped into Anna's face.

"Nice!" Anna said. "Woop! Look out—stairs ahead!"

With a bump, the bike lurched down a spiral staircase. It wobbled and bumped on the steps, but Anna and Elsa held on tightly, laughing the whole time.

"Achoo!" Elsa sneezed.

Several more little snowmen appeared, tumbling down the stairs behind Anna and Elsa. Unnoticed, the little snowmen dashed outside and raced into the courtyard.

7

Kristoff was getting worried. He and Sven had worked hard to get the courtyard ready for Anna's big birthday bash. But then the little snowmen had arrived. Every time Kristoff turned around, there were more of them.

"Where are they coming from?" Kristoff asked. Sven tossed his head and snorted.

"Does it matter?" Olaf said. "They're so fun!" He was having a blast with them.

Kristoff wasn't sure that "fun" was the

right description. The little snowmen were racing around the courtyard. They climbed onto the tables and skidded across the tablecloths, and they had already knocked over several flower arrangements.

Then some of them started clambering up the ladder. Another group was climbing an ice pillar next to the tables. Kristoff had a sudden feeling of dread.

"Oh, no! Don't knock down the banner!" he called.

But the tiny snowmen were already pulling themselves along the banner, knocking the letters from side to side.

Kristoff grimaced. "Definitely *not* fun," he said. Then he heard Olaf talking to some of the snowmen nearby.

"Do you want to see the cake?" Olaf said.

The cake! Kristoff swung around and saw

Olaf leading several little snowmen toward the big cake. Their cute little eyes grew wide.

"No cake!" Kristoff said. Queen Elsa specifically asked me to guard that cake."

"Oops, I forgot!" Olaf said. He turned to the snowmen. "Okay, no cake. You'll have to look later."

But the little snowmen had already seen the cake.

Trying to help, Sven galloped across the courtyard and stopped in front of the cake. He lowered his head and shook his antlers, trying to block the parade of tiny snowmen. But they ran around him.

Kristoff grabbed three little snowmen who were sliding on a frozen fountain and dropped them to the ground. Then he turned and stretched—and barely caught the punch bowl before it toppled to the ground.

He ran over to Sven, who was scrambling backward, still trying to push the little snowmen aside. Kristoff and Sven stood together in front of the cake, guarding it.

"I've got your back, buddy," Kristoff told Sven.

Anna and Elsa were still giggling as they followed the birthday string down to the docks by the fjord.

"I can't wait till you see this present!" Elsa said. "Just a little bit farther."

Anna followed the string to a rowboat, which had been pulled up onto the dock. Grinning, she spotted her next present lying next to the boat.

"A fishing pole!" Anna held it up excitedly. "Elsa, will you go fishing with me?"

"Achoo!" Elsa sneezed.

Behind her, a flurry of little snowmen appeared once again. They toppled into the rowboat, which tipped back and slid into the water. Neither Anna nor Elsa saw the gang of little snowmen trying to pick up the oars and row away.

Anna turned to her sister. "Elsa, I'm starting to worry about you."

"Come on," Elsa said. "The next surprise is even better!" She clapped her hands and started off toward the center of town.

They walked along the sunbaked cobblestones. Flowers cascaded from a few window boxes, and butterflies danced in the breeze.

"I love summer," Anna said.

"I love winter," Elsa said.

Then they looked at each other and said

at the same time, "Me too!" Giggling, they gave each other a squeeze.

"Look!" Anna said. "The string is leading us into the marketplace! Elsa, how did you ever manage this?"

It was true; the string led right through the marketplace, which was bustling with activity. There were vendors everywhere, selling colorful kites and cold drinks, saddles and hayrides, fresh cheeses, and warm pies.

Anna was so busy trying to follow her birthday string that she nearly tripped over the candle maker and his wagon.

"Whoops! Sorry," Anna said. "I didn't see you. I'm following this string, and—"

"Princess Anna!" the candle maker exclaimed. "It's your birthday today, yes? May I present you with a candle to celebrate?"

"Wow, thank you," Anna replied. She

plucked a bright yellow candle from his basket. "How did you know it was my birthday?"

"We all know—"

"How nice!" Elsa interrupted. The candle maker had created special candles for Anna's party. But Anna wasn't supposed to know that—at least, not yet. "Everyone knows when it's the princess's birthday," Elsa added hastily.

"Oh, right!" Anna said. "I mean, they do? They know it's my birthday?"

Elsa pushed Anna toward the glassmaker. He politely showed the sisters some new vases he had made.

But there was one special item in his display, and the string led right to it.

"Oh, look!" the queen said. *"Achoo!"*

Behind Elsa, several more little snowmen

 Elsa is throwing Anna a surprise birthday party. Even the little ice statue on top of the cake must be perfect.

Kristoff and Sven hang the birthday banner.

 Elsa tiptoes into Anna's room.
It's time to wake the birthday girl!

Elsa creates a special new dress for Anna.

Elsa gives Anna lots of gifts, but they're all hidden. Anna must
follow a string that Elsa wound through the kingdom.

As Anna gathers gifts, Elsa starts sneezing—
and they're not ordinary sneezes.

 Olaf hugs his new little brothers.

The little snowmen cause big trouble.
Luckily, Kristoff and Olaf know how to work together.

A children's choir performs for Anna, but Elsa can't stop
sneezing. Neither sister notices the little snowmen.

Olaf must rehang the birthday banner.
Too bad he can't read or spell!

The last gift on Anna's birthday tour is at the top of the clock tower. Elsa feels feverish, but she tries to hide it from Anna.

Finally, Elsa collapses. Anna rushes to her sister's side.

When Anna and Elsa reach the castle,
they run into the biggest surprise of all!

Anna is thrilled by everything—the party, the cake,
and Kristoff's unexpected birthday greeting.

 Elsa worries that she ruined Anna's birthday. Anna says she loved the gifts and the party, but she loves her sister even more.

Kristoff helps the little snowmen find a new home!

appeared and ran away. Neither Anna nor Elsa saw them.

Elsa stepped behind the counter and picked up the special gift. Gently, she presented it to Anna: a snow globe.

Anna hugged her sister. The snow globe was perfect, and so beautiful—just like Elsa.

The little snowmen scampered through the marketplace.

"But that's not all!" Elsa said. She pulled Anna along by the hand until they reached a little kiosk not far away. Wandering Oaken had brought his goods—and his sauna— down to the marketplace!

Elsa ran to the kiosk and pulled an item from his display. "One of Oaken's 'cloakens' for you!" she told Anna.

Anna twirled the beautiful heavy cloak around and hugged it tight. "I love it . . . but your cold is getting worse, Elsa," she said.

"I don't get colds," Elsa protested. But she didn't sound certain. She looked at Oaken's steamy sauna and impulsively opened the door. She took a deep breath of steamy air to help unclog her nose. "Ahhhh . . ."

"Are you sick?" Oaken asked from the doorway, surprising the sisters. The big man was barely visible in all the steam. "Perhaps you would like to try a remedy of my own invention?" Oaken held up a bottle of homemade medicine.

"No, thanks," Elsa said, and she left the sauna, eager for Anna to continue discovering her surprises.

"We'll take it," Anna told Oaken. She grabbed the cold remedy and raced after her sister.

8

As she followed Elsa, Anna nearly stumbled over a small child. It was the same girl Elsa had encountered the day before.

"I'm sorry!" she said. "Are you okay?"

"Yes," the little girl replied. "My name is Kirsten, and I'm about to sing for Princess Anna. It's her birthday today!"

"You are? It is?" Anna said. By this time, Anna was overloaded with presents, and Kirsten clearly didn't recognize the princess behind all the packages.

"Yes," the little girl said. "My mama put my hair in braids because today is special. Princess Anna is my favorite. Which one do you like better, Princess Anna or Princess Elsa?"

"Well, hmm. I think I like Elsa best." Anna turned her face away to hide her smile.

"I have to go now," Kirsten told her. "Will you be at our concert?"

"I'm pretty sure I will!" Anna said.

Kirsten ran off to catch up with several other schoolchildren gathering on a platform in the middle of the square. Anna saw that Elsa was standing in front of them with her hands in the air.

Just as someone guided Anna to her seat of honor, Elsa began to conduct the choir! The children were singing a special song that had been written just for Anna's birthday.

In the third row of the choir, Kirsten stood with her jaw dropped. She was staring right at Anna, who now sat in her appointed chair. Clearly Kirsten had just realized that she was Princess Anna!

Anna waved at Kirsten and smiled. The little girl waved back shyly.

Anna shifted her mound of gifts, which had been steadily growing. She was still carrying the cuckoo clock, the portrait, the fishing rod, the cloak, the snow globe, and—whoops! She almost dropped everything!

"Achoo!" Elsa sneezed again and blew her nose. Several little snowmen appeared, landing right on the stage with the choir. The sisters didn't see them, but the children did. The little snowmen ran around the stage, causing great excitement.

"Please, Elsa," Anna said, a note of

concern in her voice. "You need to rest. You're getting sick!"

But once again, Elsa refused. When the song was over, she pushed Anna along toward her next birthday surprise.

Behind them, the choir children happily chased the little snowmen.

Kristoff was still doing his best to keep Anna's birthday surprise safe from the little snowmen. But every time he turned around, more of them were piling into the courtyard! They raced around and nearly knocked Kristoff over. They were even climbing into the shape of a small pyramid in their attempts to reach Anna's cake.

"No!" Kristoff shouted. "STAY AWAY FROM THAT CAKE!"

Seeing Olaf nearby and desperate for an idea, Kristoff grabbed the snowman's head off his body. "Thanks in advance, buddy," Kristoff whispered.

"Uh-oh," Olaf said.

Kristoff wound up his arm and rolled Olaf's head like a bowling ball. It tumbled across the courtyard and knocked down the pyramid with a thud.

"Yes!" Kristoff pumped his fist.

Next to him, Olaf's headless body jumped into the air, and one of his little twig arms gave Kristoff a fist-bump.

"Nice!" Olaf's head shouted from across the courtyard. The cake was saved again.

Kristoff was careful to put Olaf's head back onto his body.

"Thanks," Olaf said.

Then Kristoff turned to see several little

snowmen knocking down the birthday banner. All the letters fluttered to the ground.

"I can fix it!" Olaf exclaimed.

Kristoff didn't have a choice. He had to protect the cake, so he left Olaf with the banner letters.

Kristoff turned to face several little snowmen who were charging at the cake.

"No!" Kristoff scolded.

The little snowmen stopped charging, but they still ignored Kristoff. They piled onto a table and started pelting him with snowballs. Kristoff grabbed an empty punch bowl and placed it upside down on his head as a helmet.

"Now stand back!" Kristoff said triumphantly.

But the snowmen refused. The little guys ran straight at Kristoff and knocked him to the ground. *"Oof!"* Kristoff grunted.

Behind him, Olaf proudly announced that the birthday banner was ready. "All fixed!" he called out.

Kristoff stared at the newly rearranged letters of the banner and read it aloud. "DRY BANANA HIPPY HAT?" he said, confused.

Olaf grinned. "See? We just need to clean up a little, and everything will be okay." He hugged one of the little snowmen. "Aren't you cute?"

"They are not cute!" Kristoff yelled.

Elsa's nose was stuffy, her eyes were watering, and she couldn't stop sneezing. But she was too excited to end the treasure hunt now. She led Anna to the bottom of Arendelle's clock tower. When she looked

up to the top, she felt exhausted. But after taking a big breath, she waved her little sister over.

"Come on," she told Anna. "Now we climb."

Anna peered up at Elsa from under her latest birthday present: a big hat with birthday candles burning all around its rim. She was completely loaded down with presents, but that wasn't what worried her the most.

"You want to climb all the way to the top?" She blew out a candle on the edge of the hat and shifted her load of birthday presents. "Elsa, that's too much. You need to rest."

Elsa shivered. Was it excitement, or—

"I think you have a fever!" Anna said.

"I'm fine, Anna, really," Elsa said as she began climbing the steps. "Absolutely . . . fine." Her feet felt very heavy. But she was anxious to show Anna the next gift. "I'm going to make sure that this time you don't miss out on any birthday chills—I mean, *thrills.*"

Anna was really starting to worry. Elsa had been sneezing so much, and now she looked unsteady on her feet. Her face was flushed. Elsa was usually so composed and calm. Something was not right. Anna had never seen Elsa get sick, but did that mean she *couldn't* get sick?

Still, there didn't seem to be any way to stop Elsa's excitement. Anna took a deep breath, hoisted her presents onto her shoulder, and followed Elsa up the steps into the clock tower.

9

Inside the castle courtyard, Kristoff was still battling the little snowmen. They seemed intent on getting to Anna's birthday cake. Plus, more and more kept arriving! Were they multiplying? What was going on?

Sven chased several of them away from the cake. He ran after them as they scampered back and forth among all the statues and pillars in the courtyard. Sven couldn't move quite as fast as the little snowmen, but he did his best to block them with his antlers.

Scooting happily away, the little snowmen slid along icy patches and careened around the frozen fountains. But when they rounded an icicle post, Sven couldn't make the sharp turn after them. Panting, the big reindeer crashed right into the post. His tongue stuck to the icy pole.

"Hi, Sven!" Olaf said. "Do you need some help?"

Sven looked at Olaf helplessly.

"Mfff," Sven snorted.

"Oh, what?" Olaf said. "I can't understand you. Maybe you should take your mouth away from that pole—"

Just then three little snowmen rammed into Olaf. He spun around in a circle and his head almost flew off.

"Ahhh!" he cried.

The little snowmen ran past him.

Then four more little snowmen sped around Olaf. He held on to his head and then lifted it into the air as his body spun in circles. When the spinning stopped, he dropped his head back into place.

Olaf paused and looked around, turning his head and testing his view. "I think I'm good," he noted.

Over by the cake table, Kristoff was having his own problems. "Please!" he shouted. "Just—no! Stay away from the cake!"

But seven little snowmen had finally clambered up onto the cake table. Desperate, Kristoff dove toward the table, then picked up the cake and held it as high in the air as he could. The cake's four layers tipped from one side to the other as he tried to balance it.

"Stop!" Kristoff shouted. The little snowmen surrounded him and tried to climb up his body. "Whoa! Oh, hey! Ticklish! Hee, hee."

Kristoff broke free of the little snowmen, but only for a second. He began to run and tripped over other little snowmen.

As Kristoff fell, he managed to hold the cake up high. He tossed it toward Olaf before he hit the ground.

"Hey-oh!" Olaf called out cheerfully. He had lost his head again, and he watched the cake fly through the air. His body was about three feet away, and he lifted his little twig arms to catch the cake.

Nearby, Sven's tongue was still stuck to the ice pole. He looked up with a worried expression.

The cake spiraled toward Olaf, but . . .

"*Nooooo!*" Kristoff said.

The cake flew over the heads of several

little snowmen. It flew over Olaf. Then it headed toward Sven—and miraculously, the reindeer caught the cake in his antlers.

"What a catch, Sven! Good boy!" Kristoff said. Then he saw something out of the corner of his eye. He turned and saw a bunch of little snowmen swinging from the birthday banner!

"Now hold on!" Kristoff said. Then he stopped short. The banner panels had been rearranged again. It now read: HAPPY HAIRY ANT BAND.

Kristoff groaned. How would they ever keep things in good shape until Anna's surprise party?

"Phew! There sure are a lot of steps in here," Anna said as she lugged the cuckoo clock, portrait, fishing rod, cloak, and snow globe up the stairwell of the clock tower.

Clang! Clang! The clock tower's bell was ringing in the hour.

"Wow, it's really loud in here," said Anna. "I have never been here when it's ringing!"

Elsa's face was flushed. Her head was pounding, her fever was rising, and her nose was getting stuffier. "You're going to love your next present!" she told Anna.

"I know I will," Anna said. "But, Elsa? Are you okay?"

"What?" Elsa's head was spinning. She really, really wanted this day to be perfect. Anna deserved it, and Elsa refused to give up on her plan, not now.

Elsa's thoughts drifted back to the days when she and Anna were just little girls and nothing had gotten in the way of their fun times together. Elsa could even remember when Anna was born! It seemed as if the entire kingdom of Arendelle had celebrated her arrival.

It had been nighttime when Elsa was finally allowed to see her mother and her new baby sister. The fjord was filled with ships and boats. They were lit up to celebrate the birth of the tiny new princess. Some of the people of Arendelle even launched fireworks into the night sky. The fjord seemed to sparkle with delight.

The first thing Elsa noticed about her little sister was her thick crop of orange-red hair.

"Her head is so bright!" Elsa said. "Will it shine at night?"

Her parents had laughed softly. "No, no," the queen said. "Anna has red hair. That's all."

As Anna grew, so did Elsa's powers. Elsa loved to make ice crystals that danced in the sunlight and cast sparkles on the ceiling over baby Anna's crib. Elsa delighted her little sister. She painted the little girl's windows with snowflakes and turned her fruit juices into icy parfaits.

Over time, Anna learned to walk and talk.

The two sisters began to make snow angels in their bedrooms, and later, they sneaked downstairs to play in the amazing winter wonderlands that Elsa made in the ballroom.

Then the accident had happened. And Elsa had learned to hide as she tried desperately to control her powers. During all that time, the family rarely celebrated birthdays or anything else. . . .

"Elsa?" Anna asked again, louder. "Are you okay?"

"Fine! Yes, I'm fine!" Elsa replied, wiping her brow. It certainly was getting hot. "I was just remembering how cute you were as a baby."

"Really?" Anna asked. "You don't need to—"

"Surprise!" Elsa reached the top of the stairs. There was a door that opened onto a ledge in front of the giant clock face.

Elsa held up the birthday string. At the other end of it were two wooden dolls—they looked just like Anna and Elsa! The craftsmanship was amazing.

Elsa and Anna walked out onto the ledge and looked at the dolls. Around them, the view was incredible. The sisters could see all of Arendelle from their high perch. But Elsa seemed to be swaying.

"Please be careful, Elsa," Anna said.

"Now I'm going to sing for my little sister!" Elsa's voice was loud, but it quavered, as if she wasn't quite sure what she was singing. Then she twirled, trying to make a flourish . . . but instead, she lost her balance and started to fall.

"Whoa!" Anna cried. She dropped her presents and rushed to catch Elsa. "Look at you—you're burning up! Elsa, you're so feverish!"

Anna had loved the day so far, but enough was enough. The queen was ill.

Elsa sighed and slowly nodded. She had to admit the truth: she had a cold and needed to go to bed.

Anna helped Elsa back down the clock tower stairs. Elsa had gone from being totally in control to barely being able to walk.

"Can I carry some of your gifts for you?" Elsa asked, leaning on Anna.

Anna shook her head. "Let's just worry about carrying *you*."

To make things easier, Anna left her presents along the stairs. She knew she could return for them later that day, or the next day, or even the day after that. It was too hard to carry a delicate snow globe *and* help her big sister. Anna knew which was more important.

"So this is a cold?" Elsa asked. "Are colds contagious? I've never had one before."

"Yes, and yes. And really?" Anna said.

"Well, you know, I've never been bothered by the cold."

"That's true."

"I don't think I love *having* a cold, though," Elsa added.

When they reached the bottom of the stairwell, Anna helped Elsa through the town square and toward the castle.

"I'm sorry, Anna," Elsa said. "I just wanted to give you one perfect birthday, but I ruined it. Again." This definitely was not how she had wanted Anna's birthday to be.

"You didn't ruin anything," Anna said. "Everything has been absolutely perfect."

Anna noticed that the town square seemed very quiet.

"Good thing it's quiet," Anna said. "That will help you take a nap."

As the two approached the castle gates, Elsa leaned on Anna. She was having a hard time concentrating. But the party was still on . . . wasn't it? Elsa wondered how poor Kristoff was doing with the preparations. At least Anna would have a nice cake. . . .

Together, the sisters walked up to the castle gates. Anna patted her sister's arm. "Here we are!" she said.

Anna leaned her back against the gates and pushed.

As the gates swung open, Elsa could see over Anna's shoulder into the courtyard beyond. Her mouth fell open in dismay.

11

Behind Anna, Elsa could see little snowmen everywhere: on the ground, on the tables, and even on Olaf. And the cake she had been so proud of was being tossed back and forth from Olaf to Sven to Kristoff to keep it away from the snowmen.

As the little snowmen jumped at the cake, poor Kristoff scrambled onto Sven's shoulders, holding the cake as high in the air as he could, to keep it safe. "No, no!" he cried through the chaos. "Please! Stop!"

A crowd of little snowmen had encircled one of the frozen columns, where Sven was balancing precariously. Kristoff had climbed atop Sven's antlers. Kristoff's arms were over his head, holding up Anna's birthday cake.

In front of Elsa, Anna turned around to see what her sister was looking at.

At that moment, everyone froze, and the birthday banner fluttered back into place. Somehow, it even spelled out the correct message: HAPPY BIRTHDAY ANNA!

Elsa looked at her sister and then back at the courtyard. Nothing was as she had left it, but oddly, everything seemed okay.

"SURPRISE!" shouted a chorus of voices.

Anna's face lit up in amazement. "Wow!" she exclaimed.

"Wow?" Elsa echoed.

"Happy birthday!" Olaf shouted. Kristoff,

Sven, and all the little snowmen joined him as they cheered and started to sing. Despite the chaos and the swarms of little snowmen, they had somehow pulled off Anna's birthday surprise.

As everyone sang, Kristoff slid off Sven's antlers and carried the cake toward Anna. He was so relieved and pleased that the celebration had worked, he sang louder than anyone.

Twirling, he slid to a stop right in front of Anna and held the cake out to her. And he sang dramatically, *"Happy birthday, Anna, I love you!"*

Anna's eyes widened in surprise. *Did he just say that?* she thought.

Kristoff looked stunned, too. Then he shrugged and smiled.

Then Sven sliced the cake with his antlers

and everyone had a piece. It truly was a perfect day in so many ways.

"Now," Anna told Elsa firmly, "to bed with you." The cake was wonderful and the party was fun, but Anna knew her sister needed rest.

Elsa had one more objection . . . even though she was exhausted, and a soft pillow sounded like heaven. "Wait!" she said. "One last thing! The queen needs to blow the birthday horn!" Elsa wanted to finish Anna's birthday with an official blast.

"Oh, no, no!" Anna tugged on her sister's arm. "Come on!"

But Elsa dug in her heels. She ran to the royal birthday horn and, with help, lifted the huge horn to her lips. She blew into it as hard as she could. . . .

"*Ahh-CHOOOOOOO!*" Elsa sneezed into

the horn, and the sound echoed. It was the biggest birthday blast ever heard in the kingdom of Arendelle!

This time, Elsa's sneeze did not create little snowmen. It created a giant, enormous, tremendous . . . snowball. The snowball launched into the air, high above Arendelle. It careened over mountains, across the ocean, and over almost an entire continent.

Finally, the snowball lost momentum and started to drop down over a distant island.

At that very moment, Prince Hans of the Southern Isles happened to be busy in the royal stables, shoveling manure. Hearing a whistling sound, he looked up just in time to see a huge snowball hurtling across the sky.

"Whoa!" said Hans.

The snowball took a sudden turn downward—and slammed onto Hans!

The handsome prince was knocked backward with such force that he fell into a wheelbarrow full of horse poo. *SPLAT!*

Back in Arendelle, Anna finally managed to put Elsa to bed. She helped Elsa sit up against her pillow, and then carried over a mug of hot soup. Holding it carefully, she helped her sister take a sip.

Elsa looked up gratefully. It felt so good to rest.

Anna smiled at her sister. "Best birthday present ever, you know."

Elsa thought for a second. "Which one?"

Anna pulled the heavy Oaken "cloaken" over her sister. "You letting me take care of you."

EPILOGUE

High up on the North Mountain, miles above Arendelle, Marshmallow was inside Elsa's frozen palace. The huge snowman heard a knock on the front door.

Marshmallow's heavy footsteps rumbled through the empty palace as he walked over and pulled open the door.

Outside, Kristoff, Sven, and Olaf stood at the top of the icy staircase leading into the palace.

"Hi, Marshmallow!" Olaf said. "Did you miss me?"

And with that, Olaf breezed into the

palace . . . followed by hundreds of little snowmen. "You're going to love this place!" Olaf told the little guys.

Olaf stopped next to Marshmallow and waved at all the tiny snowmen as they crowded through the door. "This way, Sludge," Olaf called. "And Slush and Slide and Ansel and Flake and Fridge and Flurry and Frost and Powder . . ." He had named every single one!

Kristoff stood just outside, leaning against the door with a tired look on his face. Glancing at a confused Marshmallow, Kristoff rolled his eyes. "Don't ask," he advised, shaking his head.